A DAUGHTER WHO FOUND HER WAY

CHIKIYA BALTHROP

DISCLAIMER

This is the past as I remember it.

To maintain the privacy of people still living, in some instances I have changed the names of individuals and places, and identifying characteristics and details such as physical properties, dates, and places of residence.

For God, who made me who I am today.

For my mom and my grandpas, who helped Him out a lot!

TABLE OF CONTENTS

Disclaimer

INTRODUCTION

Have you ever felt not good enough? Have you felt lonely, scared, or empty?

Have you felt like you have to bend over backward to be liked or loved? Have you ever felt pressured to do something that felt wrong to you? Like you had to do it to gain someone's approval? Have you ever wanted to fit in, but felt unable to do so?

Have you ever wondered why your relationships just aren't working?

You're not alone. I've felt that way, too. I'm

here to tell you it's alright. You don't have to be afraid anymore.

We live in a culture where we constantly seek our affirmations from the world and others. Why is it that we seek so much in the world when God is there to love us with open arms?

You don't have to struggle to be liked or loved. God loves you already. The Creator of the Universe loves you because you're His child. What could be better than that?

God loves you just the way you are. After all, He made you that way. He made you like yourself, and not like anyone else. And He did it for a reason.

We live in a culture where it sometimes seems like we are everyone's helpers. We try to soothe others when they're feeling bad and feed them when they're hungry. We want to be the image of God to all people: unconditionally loving, supportive, and forgiving.

That desire is wonderful. We are made to help

others, just like we're made to be ourselves. But we often forget the other side of the equation.

We're not the *only* ones responsible for living in God's image. We deserve to be loved unconditionally, too. We deserve to be loved, just as we are. Just like we love others.

What does it mean to surround ourselves with others who treat us as well as we treat them? What does it mean to stand up and say that we are worthy of love, and worthy to be treated as the sacred children of God that we are?

All too often, our divine desire to love others can turn into a human craving for approval. Into the idea that righteous behavior isn't treating all creatures—ourselves included—as children of God, but rather doing whatever those around us ask of us. We can find ourselves feeling, and behaving, as though we owe others the world. But it's often much harder to expect others to show us the same respect.

It took me a long time to learn that I am made in God's image, just as much as everyone else. He made me to love others—but also to love myself.

I am loved and worthy of love. I don't have to win love by pleasing others. I only have to live out God's image and likeness by doing what's right—whether it's popular or not.

Walking the straight line isn't easy. It can be hard to say "no" to anything without feeling guilty, when you really want to help people. It requires tough choices.

Choosing to spend time with good people can be hard. Choosing not to spend time with those who don't treat you right can feel "mean" or "selfish" or "judgmental."

But God didn't make us to be treated badly. He made us to not only show His unconditional loving nature to the world—but also to experience it from others, the way that we deserve.

So often, we become lost seeking our identity in approval from the world. This often leaves us feeling lost, frustrated, and mistreated by others.

There is another way. When we seek out our identity in God, He will never mistreat us.

We are all God's children. And we all deserve to be treated like it.

This book is not just about being loving, but about learning to be loved.

It's a journey through my walk with God, and how even though I ran from Him, I found my way back.

CHAPTER 1

Who remembers their earliest years of life? Just about no one. This effect even has a name: infantile amnesia.

Scientists say we lose access to almost all our memories of what happened to us before the age of three. But those memories don't lose access to *us*.

Instead, we continue to be shaped by the earliest events in our lives. Our adult relationships mirror our expectations from these early years. Even when we're very small—too small to remember—doctors can predict our adult relationships by looking at how we have already learned to interact with others.

Did we learn that people are trustworthy or untrustworthy? Do we expect to be taken care of, or are we afraid that might not happen? Did we learn that we can expect to be loved, or that we'd have to work hard to be deserving of love?

I don't remember my earliest years. So I'll leave this chapter blank, for you to fill in later. Let's see what my later life tells us about what I learned in my introduction to the world.

CHAPTER 2

"Okay, Chikiya, it's time for church." My aunt held out her hand to me, smiling. I knew that my mom couldn't come with us—her job made her work on Sundays—but my aunt, uncle, cousin, brother and I piled into a caravan of cars together to go to my grandpa's church every Sunday.

My grandpa was a pastor. He seemed to be able to help just about anybody. He was calm and collected, bringing certainty and confidence to uncertain situations. He was kind and humble, bringing warmth and love wherever he went. He was wise and learned, connecting people to God's word when they spoke with him. I didn't quite understand how and why, but I knew that my grandpa was *good*.

I knew I wanted to help people. I knew I wanted to be like him.

I remember him gathering the family around, putting his hands on my aunt and uncle's back and drawing us in close for a prayer. The whole family gathered around, and we could feel the energy—the warmth and heat of that moment, the power that seemed to be there with us.

"Dear Lord, please help Mrs. Janice," my grandpa prayed. "Please take the sickness from her. I know You have a plan for her, Lord. I know that everything that happens serves Your purpose. And I know Your purpose for Mrs. Janice is a loving one. Please show us what it is."

When Mrs. Janice walked into church two weeks later and gave testimony about how God had healed her, I was impressed. I was all the more certain that I wanted to be like my grandpa.

But how, exactly, did I do that? What allowed him to be so calm and collected, and yet so humble and kind?

At church on Sundays, my grandpa wore his dark-blue robe. I never saw anybody wearing robes except at church, and I knew that they were special. I knew they set people apart from ordinary people.

I knew that people gathered around these folks in robes for very important reasons, and that folks came from miles around to see them. But I didn't quite understand why.

As the adults prepared for the service to begin on Sundays, the other children and I would sit in the back of the church. Our teachers—a pair of older ladies wearing their best Sunday hats and dresses— would hand us little pamphlets with words and pictures on them.

I'd stare at the illustrations of Adam and Eve, Noah's Ark, and Moses parting the Red Sea. I'd memorize the stories and the words in the pamphlets and get praised for doing so, but I didn't really understand *why* I was doing it?

What did Adam and Eve, or Noah's Ark, or Moses parting the Red Sea mean for me? What did it have to do with my life?

Sunday school felt like sitting in science class. Okay, fine, this is where I came from. But why should I care?

What does it mean that God made me, and all the animals and plants? *Why* do we pray to God, other than to be told we're doing a good job by our parents and teachers?

I never had the courage to ask, because it seemed like I should already know. Everyone agreed that praying and reading the Bible was good—what was wrong with me? Why didn't I understand *why*?

I didn't want to ask why, because I didn't want

to be seen as bad or stupid. Everyone agreed that religion was good. It was just what you *did*. I felt like everybody else instinctively knew the reason why, and I was the one who had missed something. I was too scared to ask for it to be explained to me.

When kids are taught religion this way, it's easy to see why they leave it later in life. Praising someone for being well-behaved only works on children. When we don't understand *why* the rules exist, why the stories are important, what they tell us about what our lives are supposed to be like—why would we stick with them as adults?

Too many people talk about religion just in terms of facts. *What happened in the Bible? Look how many scripture verses I have memorized.*

But too many people can't answer the *why*.

I knew that my grandpa's religion was related to his kindness. I knew that the Bible said we were supposed to be good and kind. I figured that was why he did it. That, maybe, was why the Bible was important.

So I'd study it hard. I'd sit frowning with concentration, bent over my illustrated children's Bible, memorizing as many words as I could. But so many scriptures—I didn't see how they were related to my life, or to what my grandpa did.

I'd kneel beside my bed every night, knees on the carpet and my elbows resting on my soft, fluffy comforter. I'd recite, softly:

"Now I lay me down to sleep
I pray the Lord my soul to keep
If I should die before I wake
I pray the Lord my soul to take"

I'd look up at the ceiling—try to look through it—since the sky was where God was supposed to be.

My family said that saying those words made me good, but who exactly was I talking to?

CHAPTER 3

"Did you have fun with your dad?" my mom asked, as my brother Justin bounded up our front steps and pushed open our screen door.

My brother was so lucky. He knew his dad. I knew that my dad was in the military, but that was about it. We never went out for barbecues, and I didn't have a whole other gaggle of aunts and uncles and siblings like he did. I didn't get to go on adventures with my dad every other weekend.

I didn't know where I came from.

And so, twice a month, I watched Justin get picked up by his whole other, happy family, and go off and have adventures without me. He always left and came back smiling, full of stories of the fun times they'd had.

I'd never met my own dad, and I wanted to know *why*.

Lots of people think that if a child never has a dad, she won't miss him. That being in a single-parent household will just be "normal" for her. But kids have eyes. I knew that most children had something I didn't. They had at least *met* their dad, or spent time with him every now and then.

My mom said my dad was a good man, and that he cared about me. She said I had a big sister through him: a girl named Yara, who I had never met. She said he paid child support, but because of his job in the military, she didn't know where he was. I wasn't sure why he never called.

My mom said that my dad was in the military, and that meant he had to go far away for a long time. But eleven years? In eleven years, I had never met my father. He'd had time to pay child support, apparently, but not to talk to me.

I didn't recognize, at the time, that I was craving to learn where I came from. I knew I was sad that my brother had a dad and I didn't, and that I longed for fun times like he had with his dad's side of the family. But I didn't know that I wanted to know about where—about *who*—I came from.

I just knew I wanted answers. And that some part of me, deep down, wanted to know what it was like to be a "daddy's girl." I wanted to know what it was like to have my father in my life. To have him there.

I was afraid to ask my mom much more about my dad. I was afraid that if I kept asking about him, she'd feel like she wasn't enough for me.

I was also a little bit afraid to learn the truth. Had he hurt her feelings, and run off? Had he left because he didn't want me?

Still, I saw kids all over the place with fathers. I saw kids on TV learning who their fathers were.

I was about eleven when I realized how I could find my dad without needing to keep asking my mom questions. I'd watched a talk show where a woman met her own father for the first time as an adult, and I'd seen how she'd done it.

Like the woman on that show, I'd look at my birth certificate and see who was listed as my father there.

I waited until my mother was away at work and my brother was out with his dad. Then, when I was sure I would not be spotted, I crept into my mom's room, where I knew all the family documents were kept.

My heart pounded with excitement and I broke

into a cold sweat as I looked around my mother's room. Mysterious boxes lined the walls. They were stowed under the desk and in the closet. It seemed like any of those might have contained papers.

I had no idea where she kept the family records. But for a document as important as a birth certificate, the pile of papers neatly stacked on her desk seemed a good place to start.

The act of rooting through the files, looking for my name, felt forbidden. I imagined how I would explain myself if my mother walked in the room.

But at last, there it was. My own name, written in my mom's neat handwriting on a beige folder.

Inside this folder were the answers—but was I ready for them?

My heart crept into my throat as I opened it.

Chikiya Balthrop, the certificate read, my name written for the very first time in someone's graceful, looping handwriting.

Mother: Jenetta Balthrop.

Father: Edward Foster.

I stared at the name, not knowing what to do with it. It was just a name. It could have belonged to anyone.

Who was Edward Foster? What was he like? Did I get my looks from him? My personality?

And just like that, I knew how I would find out.

"Army Recruiter's Office, how can I help you?"

The man on the other end of the line sounded so strong. So official. So *forceful*. I didn't know what to say to him.

"Hi…" I heard how young I sounded, how uncertain. And I hated it. I didn't want to sound like the child that I was. Not now. Not while I had a job to get done.

"My name is Chikiya Balthrop," I said, mustering all the confidence I could. "I'm looking for my father. I know his name is Edward Foster, and he's in the army."

There was a long pause on the other end of the line. My heart was hammering in my chest again as I wondered if I would get in trouble.

"Miss Balthrop," the recruiter's voice came again, smooth and calm, "does your father know you're calling?"

I bit my tongue. "No. I've never met him."

"I see." His voice was gentle now. "Well, I have an email address for him here on file. Do you have an email address, too?"

My heart soared, even as my hand holding the phone shook. I managed to recite my email address for him, and imagining meeting my father, *hearing* from him, almost became too much for me. Would I have a loving dad now, just like my brother did?

"Thank you, Miss Balthrop," the man on the phone said courteously. "I'll send him your contact information."

"Th—thank you, sir," I stammered.

"You have a good day now, Miss."

He hung up.

And I stood with the phone receiver in hand, trembling.

After all these years, was I about to meet my father?

I waited for an email that never came.

At first, I eagerly checked my account as often as I could. Checking your email two or three times a day was a *lot* in the early 2000s, when most families owned only one computer, and had to connect to the Internet through a single phone line that could only be used by one person at a time. I hovered near the computer, waiting to hear from my dad—all while not daring to tell my mother what I'd done.

But then, disaster struck. My password—a random string of numbers, letters, and symbols that my email provider had assigned to me—went missing. The little slip of paper I had kept it on next to the computer was simply gone, and no one knew how to access my account.

A hole opened up in my heart. I had been so close. After the disappointment of waiting for a message that never came, I couldn't bear to try reaching out to my father again.

This pain and disappointment deep within me bubbled up until I had to do *something* with it. I didn't feel that I could talk to my mother about it, and I wasn't sure I wanted to. I knew what she'd tell me: that *she* knew my daddy loved me, and that was enough.

It didn't feel like enough.

I started to ask God for something new during my nightly prayer times.

Is it meant for me to meet my father, God? I'd ask as I stared up at the ceiling.

Is it meant for me to meet him? I'm hoping you'll say yes.

I knew that some girls my age kept a journal, so I started doing the same thing. Into this secret book, I poured my heart and my feelings—all the fears, pains, and desires I was afraid to share with anyone else. This literally became my safe place.

It was incredible how good it felt to be honest about my feelings, even if it was with a book.

I'd grown up worrying about how others would react to my words. What if I said something, and they responded by feeling sad, or scared, or like they weren't good enough? I didn't want to hurt anybody. What if I asked a question that everybody else already seemed to know the answer to? Would I seem bad, or stupid?

But I didn't have to worry about what this book thought. And though I didn't know it yet, this was a special way for me to talk to God.

So much of my life was consumed with being "good," up to that point, that I'd forgotten to be myself. I'd been a helpful daughter and a good sister and a student who memorized her Bible verses, but I hadn't really allowed myself to *feel* my feelings.

I thought I existed for the purpose of "being good." It never occurred to me that God put me here, not just to behave myself, but to *feel* and have *experiences*.

My grandfather said that God has a purpose for each of our lives. Now, I started to think more seriously about what that might mean.

As I wrote in the sacrosanct privacy of my journal, I started to understand my own feelings more. I felt my pain more keenly—and that meant I could take action to do something about it. I felt my frustrations and my fears, and that got me thinking about how to make them better.

I knew that my family always told me to pray to God. But I had only ever been taught one prayer:

Now I lay me down to sleep
I pray the Lord my soul to keep.
If I should die before I wake
I pray the Lord my soul to take.

I had grown up watching them gather around the kitchen table to offer thanks and to ask for help. But I'd thought that those were things you did because you were *supposed* to. Not because you were *feeling* something and you wanted to *express yourself.*

I may have grown up around prayer and known it as a church girl, but the idea of reaching out to God was foreign to me. I understood prayer as something you did because someone told you it was good. Prayer was a scripted series of words that you said—not a conversation.

When I journaled, though, I began to see another way of being. I started to address my journal entries to God.

In the privacy of my journal, I could ask God for what I *really* wanted. I could tell him how I really felt.

And I said to him, *"God, I want to know who my father was."*

I began to see that it was okay to say how I felt, to live in my feelings—if only in the silence of my heart.

CHAPTER 4

Years passed without word from my father. I grew up without a dad in my life. My mom considered this normal, but I looked at my brother and all my friends who *did* have fathers, and I longed for what they had.

A dad to play with them. A dad to call them in for dinner. A dad to go to their school plays. All of those things meant the world to me, when I watched other people's dads do them.

In the end, finding my father was the first prayer God answered for me.

As I continued to pour my heart out to God in my journal, with no apparent response, my faith was tested.

I remembered what my grandpa had said about Mrs. Janice, back when I was a child.

"We know You have a plan for Mrs. Janice. We know it is a loving plan. Please, show us what that plan is."

My grandpa had always said that God didn't always give you what you wanted, right when you wanted it. But he also asked for Mrs. Janice to get better, and she did.

Where was the answer to *my* prayers?

I was in my teens by the time Facebook became popular. Many of my friends flocked to the new platform, feeling like adults with their very own social media profile.

There was just one catch: my mother, worried about the uncertain new technology that was social media, didn't want me on it. She worried about cyberbullying, catfishing, and more.

The good news was, Facebook had no way of checking whether you *really* had your parents' permission. Using Facebook, I could contact almost anyone. I could open new doors that had never before existed.

One day, like any other, I logged into Facebook from my primitive smartphone. I used the phone to avoid my mother seeing my browser history and finding out what I'd been doing.

On this day, I didn't expect to find anything exciting. Just the usual—my friends sharing silly statuses about their lives.

But as the Facebook screen loaded, my eye was drawn to a little red alert in the corner of the screen. I had a new friend request. My heart jumped a little. It was always good to feel popular. I clicked on the alert.

And then, when I saw her name, my jaw dropped.

Yara Foster.

Yara Foster. Edward Foster.

The woman had sent me a message, along with the friend request:

"Hey, sister."

What I learned over the next few weeks broke my heart and healed it at the same time. I knew now that God was real: he had answered my prayer in a way that seemed like divine intervention. This was not what I had ever expected, but it worked out perfectly.

My father *had* saved my email address. It was how Yara had found me.

He'd been deployed when I called the Recruiter's Office. By the time my father was back in front of a keyboard, I'd been locked out of my email account and given up hope. He wrote to me, but I never got his emails.

My dad's family didn't stop searching for me when he was deployed to Iraq. My stepmother knew that my dad had another child, and had searched for me on Myspace before Facebook was popular.

When Facebook opened to the public, my sister Yara hoped to find me there. She must have searched for my email address and sent me a message when she found it.

Getting to know a sister, a family you've never met, is a long and awkward process. It's as awkward as talking to a stranger, yet as intimate as sitting up at night giggling under the covers. You have so many imaginings of what your sister or your father might be like. The process of finding out whether they fit that image is *awkward*.

From her profile pictures, Yara looked like me. She typed with confidence and courage, yet she was also gentle. I wondered if our father was like her. I hoped.

We messaged for days, making cautious forays into getting to know each other. She asked, very carefully, if I still wanted to know my father. I asked, just as timid, if he wanted to get to know me.

"If you want to speak to him," Yara messaged me, "here's his number. I know he wants to hear from you."

The first time I dialed his number, it was with trembling fingers. I practically exploded with excitement the first time I heard his voice. Here was this perfect stranger, someone I had never spoken to. And yet he was my father.

There was just one problem: I hadn't told my mother yet.

My mother worked so hard and did so much for us kids. She'd provided us with a roof over our heads, and had always made sure we had what we needed. I didn't want her to feel like she was not enough.

But I still needed to know more about where I came from.

"Mom…" I'd never felt as timid talking to my

mother as I did then. *Scared*, sure, when I'd done something bad and I was afraid of getting in trouble. But this wasn't fear of punishment or fear that I'd done something wrong. It was something different.

I was scared of hurting my mom's feelings.

I was too afraid to tell her face-to-face. So I didn't. Instead, I climbed out of bed early the next morning and rummaged through my desk for a pen and paper. I wrote the note carefully, with sleepy eyes and jittery hands.

Dear Mom,

I wanted to let you know I found my dad. I used my birth certificate to find out who he was and tried to contact him years ago. His daughter used the email address I sent him to find me on Facebook.

We've spoken, and he wants to meet me. I had to know where I come from. I hope you're not mad.

Love,
Chikiya

I went through the school day with my heart pounding.

What would my mother do when she read my note? How would she feel? Would she feel like she wasn't enough for me? Would she feel betrayed?

When I arrived home, I opened our front door slowly and carefully. Inside, the house was quiet.

My mother didn't say anything to me as I passed the kitchen. But my note was gone. I was sure, by the way she carefully didn't look at me, that she'd read it.

She didn't even say "hello" to me as I tiptoed through the living room and threw myself onto my bed in despair.

A terrible pit opened up in my stomach. I just about felt my soul drop through it. Was what I had done really so bad? Had I hurt my mother's feelings so much, by looking for my father?

But when my mother finally spoke to me a few

days later, this was what she said: "Oh, Chikiya, why didn't you *tell* me?"

Eventually, we both managed to explain ourselves.

It wasn't the fact that I had looked for my dad that bothered my mother. It was the fact that I hadn't been open with her about it. What had she done, she wondered, to make me so afraid? Why didn't I feel like I could talk to her about anything?

That question was hard for me to answer. She'd never gotten mad when I asked about my father—not exactly. But there was something clear in her voice, in her body language. Like she wanted to avoid it. Like she was afraid to tell me too much more.

All this time, I'd been afraid to tell her, not knowing how she'd react.

It turned out, she was too afraid to tell me because she feared that that might make me miss him more.

"Well," my mother said finally, sitting heavily across from me at the kitchen table, "all things in God's time. It must be God's time for you to meet your daddy."

CHAPTER 5

My first meeting with my dad was surreal. My parents finally spoke to each other on the phone, now that I'd spilled the secret that I'd been talking to both of them. My mother realized it was important for me to meet my father, but she didn't want to drop me into his arms after not having seen him for fifteen years. Instead, it was agreed that both families would meet: me, my brother and mother, and my dad, his wife, and my younger sister and stepbrother.

My dad's home was in Maryland, and we'd meet his family halfway at Potomac Mills. Only Yara—who had been Facebook sleuthing on my dad's behalf, but who lived in Texas—would miss the reunion.

Here was this total stranger I had never met before. I knew almost nothing about him. But when I looked into his face, I saw my own. He had my red-tinted skin tone. He had green eyes that burned out of his face and helped explain why my eyes were lighter than my mother's.

I'm made of half of you. The bizarre thought occurred to me as I watched him get out of the car to make room for me, one hand raised in a greeting that was almost shy.

I stepped out of the car in the restaurant parking lot, wearing a nice church dress I'd picked for the occasion. Silly as it is to say, I was feeling shy too.

I raised one hand from behind my back and waved a little. "Hi, Dad," I said softly.

My dad stared at me for a moment, like he couldn't believe his eyes. Then he hugged me, slowly and carefully.

He greeted my mother warmly, and then helped me get my bags into the trunk of his car.

One conversation became two. Two conversations became a weekend up north in Maryland, where my dad lived with his wife and my stepbrother. A weekend became a grander plan: I'd lived my whole life with one side of the family. It was time to get to know the other side.

I met my dad, my stepmom, and her youngest son who stayed with them. My dad also called *his* father and put me on the phone with him.

My paternal grandad and I soon became fast friends. He was a bright, supportive man who wanted nothing more than to know his granddaughter. He asked me about my feelings, my school year, my plans for my life. At the time, I wanted to go to school to become an FBI agent. I had my sights set on a criminal justice major in college that would lead to a life fulfilling the law.

As my relationship with my grandad grew over the phone, my relationship with my dad grew in person. I wasn't sure we'd ever be as close as I had imagined when I watched other kids with their dads, but just having him in my life was reassuring.

While spending time with my dad, I'd notice weird things. *Little* things. We both loved the Dallas Cowboys, even though we weren't from anywhere near Texas. We both loved watching military movies and were fascinated by military history. We both liked to put sugar in our grits.

It really was true: I was half of him. And as we spent more time together, I felt a healing begin within.

I'd never really known that I missed my father. I hadn't even known the questions to ask. But seeing him, being with him, made me realize that all sorts of questions about myself were being answered. Now I knew where so many things about me came from.

My stepmom was a fascinating woman. She kept her hair cut short and groomed impeccably, always looking like she'd just stepped out of a magazine. She wore Michael Kors shoes and other designer and brand names—but she somehow found ways to stay on a budget. A budgeting genius: that was my stepmom. She could create a million-dollar look on a middle-class budget.

It helped that she made sure to check in with me. In the first weeks after I moved in with her and my dad, she regularly asked me how I felt about how she treated me, and how things were being done around the house.

Being asked gave me the opportunity to ask

myself the same questions. What *were* my feelings? How did I feel about the way things were done? What made me happy, and what made me sad? What ways of doing things did I prefer? And *why*?

Through my stepmom getting to know me, I began to notice more of what made me happy, and what made me sad. I began to know myself—not just as my mother's daughter, but as a whole different person in a whole new place. She began to buy me a wonderful gift: new journals, blank notebooks waiting to be filled with my words. She also bought me my first study Bible—a kind of Bible I'd never seen before, with footnotes and questions for me to answer inside of it.

For a while, living with my dad was like a dream for me. Here was this man who was this huge, missing part of my life. And now I got to be around him every day. I asked him questions and watched his every move. I got to know my sister, and this woman he had married. Sometimes I wondered where I fit in with the picture of their lives—but they always made it clear that I was part of their family.

Meeting my dad didn't solve all my problems. I still had questions about who I was, and what I was put on this Earth to do. But as I continued to thank God for answering my prayer, I continued to think more about my relationship with Christ, too. I had my human dad. Now what about my Heavenly Father?

Unfortunately, life is never without challenges. My new school in Maryland was in a rougher neighborhood than my old school in Virginia. Although I got along well enough with my new classmates and made new friends, being new on the block still made me a target.

One day I was walking home from school when I noticed several other girls following me on my usually solitary walk. My heart started to pound, and I fought rising panic.

Another set of footfalls reached my ears. Then another.

Suddenly, another girl was standing in front of me on the sidewalk, blocking my way. I recognized her as an older girl from my neighborhood. As I stood still, unsure what to do, more neighborhood girls surrounded me.

"Hey, new girl," she said. "I like that backpack."

I was almost scared enough to give her the bag and run. But I already knew that wouldn't work. Three other girls had circled up behind me, and they clearly hadn't come here just to take my things. They'd come here to assert their dominance. As the new girl, I needed to learn who was boss.

"I—I don't want any trouble." I tried to shrink into myself, but I knew that wouldn't work either. They wouldn't just take my word for it, that I knew who was in charge. They had to show me.

The first girl shoved me. While I was off-balance, another girl's hand reached into my pocket and yanked out my phone and keys. My backpack was being tugged on from behind, and hard. The only way to avoid falling over was to shrug it off and let them take it.

I watched as the girl with my phone flipped it open and scanned critically through the contacts. She seemed to scroll until she found what she was looking for, and her eyes lit up. She pressed the button to initiate a call, and I could faintly hear the ringing coming from the phone's speaker. Then my heart began to pound. When a voice answered, it was my dad's.

I couldn't make out my father's words. I knew he would be furious—but he was also far away. Deployed in another state, several hours' commute by ground or air.

As I watched, the older girl hung up on him and threw my phone to the ground.

I turned to see another girl examining the contents of my backpack.

"This is a nice bag," she said. "I think I'll keep it."

My hands were trembling nervously. I wondered if I should run, or if that would just make things worse. My homework was in that bag. I wanted to fight back, but I was drastically outnumbered and outsized. On the ground, my phone rang. I saw my dad's number on the caller ID.

There was nothing I could do but turn and head for my father's house, as fast as I could.

I was still trembling while my stepmom sat me down at the kitchen table and gently asked me questions. Where was my bag? Who had done this? Why had my father called her in a panic?

I didn't know. I didn't know the other girls— just their faces, from seeing them walk by from time to time. I had no idea why they had done this.

I could tell that Wanda was thinking about what to tell me. About what to tell my mother. Around here, fighting and getting jumped was common. I'd known that for weeks—but I had hoped I could stay out of it by refusing to challenge anyone.

It seemed like there were two possibilities in this district: stay and learn to fight so that no one would ever challenge me again. Or—

Well, leave. Leaving here seemed like the only way to stay away from the other students' fists.

My dad knew he had to tell my mom about the attack. And I knew what she'd say when he did.

Sure enough, two weeks later, I was packing my things for the long drive back to Virginia.

CHAPTER 6

As the years passed, I continued to journal. Even my frank talks with my stepmom couldn't match the freedom of expression I had on those private pages, and in the silence of my heart.

Thank you, God, I wrote one day, when I realized that my prayer of meeting my dad had been answered. So much time had passed that I'd almost forgotten about my original plea—and my confusion when it hadn't come to pass.

Some small, resentful part of my mind still

wondered: *Why did it take you so long?*

But I also remembered my grandpa's mysterious words. *"We know it is a loving plan."*

What if Mrs. Janice hadn't been meant to come home from the hospital when she did? What if she had stayed sick longer?

What if I hadn't been meant to meet my dad right when I asked for the first time? How would things have been different if I'd moved up to my dad's neighborhood when I was younger and more vulnerable?

We have no way to know our "what ifs," but I was learning one thing. God works in mysterious ways. And what we wanted—maybe it wasn't always best for us to get it right when we asked.

As I got older, stronger, and more confident, my mom's worries about my safety began to ease. I blossomed from a shy young girl into a confident young woman—and by the summer before my senior year of high school, my mom felt that I could take care of myself if I went back up to Maryland again.

"This time," she said, as we sat at the kitchen table late one night, "you'll be one of the seniors. You'll be one of the oldest, most confident kids in the school—not one of the youngest, smallest freshmen."

She looked at me seriously over her mug of coffee. "Chikiya," she said, "I'm thinking about joining the military. They need my skills, and if I do that—then I can't be here to protect you, either. Your brother can go live with his dad's family, and you— you can go live with your dad."

I nodded, appreciating her logic. Deep down inside, I was relieved. The few months I'd lived in Maryland last time hadn't been enough to make up for a lifetime of not knowing my dad. My relationship with him and my stepmom was still guarded and new, and I didn't want to stop getting to know them now. There was so much more to learn.

"I'll watch my back," I promised. My blood still chilled when I thought of the sound of footsteps behind me. Why any student would do that to another—just gang up on her for no reason—I couldn't understand.

But I could also see myself, now, through the eyes of an older student. As a freshman who was new to the city, I was an easy target for any bully looking to move up in the pecking order. Now, things would be very different. My dad and stepmom had moved into a new neighborhood, and I would be attending a new high school.

I returned to Maryland a different person than I'd been when I first arrived. I'd grown older, wiser, and a little more wary. But that made me stronger. No one was going to take advantage of me again.

Or so I thought.

But as it turned out, I wasn't quite ready to recognize my worth yet. I didn't yet know who I was.

Moving to Maryland showed me everything in a new light. I saw myself more sharply, removed from the familiar backdrop of my mother's home. I saw my father, and the other half of my heritage. I also learned to see who God was in a new way.

My stepmother took us to church every Sunday, just like my grandfather had done when I was a kid. But at this church, just like in her home, I felt a little different. I felt more free.

This was not a church where I was the pastor's granddaughter, and everyone had certain expectations of me. I didn't feel the same pressure to already know the right answers without having to ask questions. I didn't uncritically assume that I had to do whatever the pastor was doing.

Instead, I observed.

The people of this church were like the people

of my grandpa's church in many ways. They gathered to celebrate, to mourn, and to sit in thoughtful contemplation. They clustered around a pastor who shared the Word of God with them, and they all seemed grateful and reliant on its guidance.

Watching the pastor and his sermons, now, as an adult, I could understand better why they felt that way. As a senior in high school, I understood the need for comfort, guidance, and certainty in a confusing, uncertain world better than I'd understood these things as a little girl. I understood the importance of having God in our lives to guide us, and how we were made to fulfill the purpose He put us here for.

The knowledge that a man loved me so much that he'd died on the cross for me left me in awe. That this man was God was even more amazing.

But I also saw other things. I saw how the friendships formed in this church were based on common values. Everyone had certain shared expectations of how they should strive to behave. That made these friendships forged in church deeper—and safer, it seemed to me—than the bonds I saw forming in my school. My churchmates shared a common set of values and goals, and they took these goals very seriously. There was a sense of covenant. There was a sense of accountability.

In school, the kids could be catty. Everything seemed to be a competition. Kindness wasn't necessarily encouraged: in fact, it was often seen as a sign of weakness. Peer pressure often turned dark, with my classmates even pressuring each other into drugs, gangs, and sex for the sake of popularity. Everybody was in a hurry to prove that they were the most adult teenagers in the school, but they didn't seem to understand what being an adult meant.

The teens I met through church seemed different. Being members of the church—and spending time there together—meant one thing. It was okay to encourage each other to be kind and to engage in self-reflection. It wasn't about who could be the strongest or the prettiest or the sexiest, but who could be the kindest, the wisest, the noblest.

Yet, at the same time, these young people were also relatable. I could talk and laugh with them, and they seemed to accept me. I felt comfortable with them.

I still felt insecure. I wanted desperately to fit in, and I wanted everyone to like me. It often seemed like this wasn't possible. Even in the church community, I often felt like people were not interested in being my friend.

Still, I reached out for friendship with *someone.*

I liked so much of what I saw at this church, but I still didn't understand why some people seemed so committed to the church community. Sure, it was great that people helped each other out. But I still wasn't sure what their public prayers were really supposed to accomplish, or why some people seemed to spend more time at church than with their own families.

My stepmom saw things differently. She already knew something I didn't, which I was about to find out.

One day while we were standing in church, toward the front, the pastor delivered a powerful message.

"You all come here today—but then you go back out into the world. And who do you become then?" He seemed to look around accusingly. "Ask yourselves: this way of life you have, is it really fulfilling you? Is it making you *happy?*"

I squirmed a little in my chair. I mostly kept myself out of the competition and the cattiness at school, focusing on my grades and my family. But just being around some of the behavior I saw at school made me uncomfortable. These teens were acting like they knew just how to become adults—but to my eyes, they were playing dangerous games of one-upmanship with each other.

Somehow I knew that I was different from most of those teens. I wanted friends and I wanted to fit in, but I just wasn't interested in the things they did. Somehow, I felt set apart.

The teens at my stepmom's church, on the other hand, were different.

They went on retreats together, where they praised and worshipped God. They had serious conversations about ethics and morality. Their chief concerns seemed to be becoming better people.

They had mentors through the church who didn't talk down to them, but who they could have open, honest conversations with. This was a whole new world to me: at home, I often didn't feel like I could express myself honestly and open up about my feelings. Here, it was suddenly possible for me to talk to an adult about my feelings and receive support.

Did I want to be like these people, if I didn't want to be like the kids at school? Nah. But then... who *did* I want to be like?

I remembered the lady who had taught me in Sunday school growing up, and I shook my head at that too. Those ladies had seemed so... sanctimonious? Like they were *good*. Well-behaved. But not necessarily wise, or kind.

No, I decided. I wanted to discover who *I* was. The pastors said I was made unique and put on Earth for a reason. What was it?

"How many of you," the pastor was asking at the altar now, "have a *personal* relationship with Jesus? I don't mean just going to church every Sunday. I mean, how many of you speak to God in your *hearts?* How many of you have a *relationship* with Christ?"

That got my attention. *Speak to God in your hearts.* I thought about my journal. About how I had cried out to God within it, and later found my father.

But... was God supposed to answer?

My heart fluttered a little at that thought. I had never seen God answer my grandpa—not in words. But had my grandpa heard Him?

Could I hear Him too, if I only knew how to listen?

"Now, we all know tomorrow isn't promised," the preacher continued. "How would it feel to die, knowing you've never really lived? Knowing that you've never really known your Creator, or His will for you, in your heart? Do you want to risk eternity in Hell—or have a relationship with God and spend eternity with Him?"

My pulse began to thrum. *To know your Creator. To know where you came from.*

"Tomorrow is not promised," he said, his voice rising to a thunderous roar. "If you were to die today, where would you spend eternity? Who wants to accept Jesus into your heart and begin a *personal* relationship with God?"

I felt faint. I'd always known that God was important. But I'd never really thought that He could be my *friend*.

And as this pastor suggested it, I felt doors open in my mind and heart. The light seemed to come flooding in.

Before I knew it, I was on my feet. The pastor was waving the people who wanted to get saved up to the altar, and my body walked up there almost of its own accord.

I remember the pastor laying his hands on my forehead. "Do you accept Jesus into your heart?" His words came to me, as though from a distance. I was already experiencing something more intimate, more immediate and real, than the physical world around me.

"I do," I said, and I felt a sense of peace in my heart.

The pastor went around to all of the people who had come up to the altar. There were half a dozen of us—old and young, from all life stages. But I was only distantly aware of them as I stood on the steps beside the altar, dazed, my entire being filling with light.

I soon found myself being ushered by a kind altar worker back into a hallway behind the altar. The others and I were led down a warm, dimly lit hall into a room filled with chairs. We were invited to sit down. Each chair had a paper laid carefully on the seat. I picked up the piece of paper, curious.

Members of the altar worker team began to sit down on the empty chairs next to each of us, speaking to us one-on-one. A woman sat down next to me.

"You have chosen to be saved today," she said, looking at me with a serious but gentle expression. The warm, yellow light from the lamps made the room feel like a family gathering. "Do you know what that means?"

"It means we'll get into Heaven for sure," I volunteered, looking up from the sheet of paper with the Bible verses in my lap.

"It does mean that." The altar worker nodded, her look approving. "But it also means very much more. Can you tell me what else?"

"It means you'll have a personal relationship with Jesus," I added.

"It does," the woman nodded, a little more delighted than before.

"And what," the altar worker asked, "does that mean?"

"It means that you can talk to Jesus in your heart," I said, smiling, "and he'll answer."

Then, we prayed the prayer of salvation together.

Heavenly Father,

I come to you in prayer

Asking for the forgiveness of my sins.

I confess with my mouth and believe with my heart

That Jesus is your Son,

And that he died on the Cross at Calvary

That I may be forgiven

And may have Eternal Life.

CHAPTER 7

B eing with the church youth group was like nothing I'd experienced before. The fellowship was warm and supportive in a way that my school relationships just weren't. The youth group was focused on what really mattered: our relationships with God, helping others, and constantly improving ourselves.

Two or three times a year, our youth group visited a retreat center in the mountains of Pennsylvania. Sitting on the bus with the other teens, hushed and expectant as the beautiful natural scenery passed us by, was something I'll never forget.

We drove for miles to get to the retreat center. After we left the metropolitan area, it was nothing but forests and rolling mountain highways: God's creation. Rays of sunlight spilled out from between the big silver-lined clouds and onto the green forests below. The sky between the clouds glowed a bright electric blue. There was nothing but forest for miles and miles. The work of human hands was barely visible here.

This was astounding to me. I'd spent my whole life between the big city and the suburbs, never imagining how wide the world was beyond the borders of my hometowns. It felt like I had entered another realm. The realm that God made.

After many hours of driving, we finally pulled onto a dirt road that led into the canopy of trees. Driving down the bumpy trail with a thick roof of pine boughs over our head felt like driving into a fantasy story.

It was almost scary. I'd never been so far from the city, or so surrounded by nature before. But when the trees broke to reveal a meadow of rolling, grassy hills with a huge, stately house perched at the forest's mouth, it looked like a castle out of a fairy tale. The peace here was palpable and seemed to lay across the land like a blanket.

Two older boys, Tyrell and Trent, got out of the bus and started helping the youth group counselor to unload our luggage. Suitcase after suitcase was pulled out of the trunk as half a dozen teens piled out of the car. All around us, other cars were pulling up. Between them, dozens of teenagers from my new church climbed out to stretch their legs in the mountain air.

As he worked, Tyrell looked at me quizzically. "Is this your first retreat?" he asked.

I nodded shyly.

"Don't worry," Tyrell said. "Trent and I will

take care of you. Hey Trent! Meet the new girl. What's your name?"

"Chikiya." Instead of holding out my hand to shake, I grabbed one of the bags sitting on top of the pile Tyrell was stacking up. Together we moved the whole car's worth of luggage into the mansion waiting at the top of the hill.

The house was beautiful. I'd never been in a house like that before. A huge, airy atrium was filled with beams of sunlight spilling in from the big window at the top. The hardwood floors and cream-colored carpets were so immaculately clean that they seemed new. At each side of the huge entrance hall, a single staircase rose up what seemed like forever to a ring of twelve, second-floor bedrooms that bordered the big open space.

"You'll be staying down here, with the other girls," a female counselor told me, catching me at the door. There turned out to be half a dozen bedrooms on the main floor as well, near the huge kitchen where five round dining tables waited to seat up to thirty people.

As I settled into the room I'd be sharing with two other girls, the experience was alien to me. I'd never been to a summer camp with my youth, so sharing a bedroom, a kitchen, a house with strangers was totally new to me. It was also kind of thrilling.

"I'm Jessica." One girl held out her hand to shake, greeting me with a big smile. "Is this your first time here?"

"Yes." It was a relief that the older teens seemed to want to look out for the newcomers. "Have you been here before?"

"Oh, definitely. It's great. There's nothing better than a full weekend full of games, praise, and worship!"

I tried to imagine it.

As a child, I'd found church boring—to me, it had mostly meant memorizing pamphlets and getting lectured by pastors and Sunday school teachers. It felt like just another type of school, where you had to earn good grades or be judged for it.

But at my new church, things were different. There was a real energy that people focused through praise and worship. The songs of praise were beautiful and sometimes haunting. There was an energy that seemed to descend on the youth group, or on the whole congregation, when we sang together. When we praised and worshipped together, sometimes my worries seemed further away.

Would this whole weekend be like that? I wondered. Would it be the best weekend of my life, or the most boring?

My question was soon answered. As we unpacked and prepared to spend the night in this new place, a counselor stuck her head in to invite us into the main room.

"The opening prayer meeting is starting in five minutes," she said. "Please don't be late!"

When my roommates and I emerged into the huge atrium, we heard the sound of acoustic guitars. A whole band was tuning up to play while the youth group counselors and mentors stood together in a circle, all holding hands with their heads bowed.

The youth group teens were gathering, standing or sitting on the floor. Without chairs or pews, I realized that we were freer to move around. Some people stretched out on the ground while others walked in wide circles, swinging their arms from side to side.

Already, I felt more free.

When the first strains of the first worship song started, my heart soared. I knew it was going to be a great weekend.

By the end of the evening prayer meeting, everyone felt warm and contented with God's presence. Singing together had already bonded us, though some of us had come in as strangers.

While the band continued to play, the counselors encouraged us to form circles with those around us to pray about the challenges we were facing. Throughout the weekend, we'd have breakout sessions with our youth mentors to discuss the things that we were facing with them.

It was eye-opening to hear about the battles that other people my age were fighting. One boy's parents were divorcing after a long marriage. One girl's mother had recently been diagnosed with cancer. As we all gathered together, we first held hands, then put our arms around each other.

We had all come here seeking solace, only to

find that we were safe and held in the community of the Lord. It was enough to bring tears to many eyes.

At the end of the night, the counselors asked us to count off in numbers one to five. Each of us would recite a number, repeating the one to five sequence until everyone in the retreat house had a number. They then announced that the people who had the same number as us were our "small group" members for the rest of the week.

At breakfast the next morning, I began to see the genius of this system. By randomly assigning us to groups, no one would be left out or struggle to fit in. As I searched for a place to sit to eat with these relative strangers, the other Number Threes enthusiastically beckoned me.

To my delight, Tyrell and Trent were at the table.

"Hey, little sister," Trent enthused as I sat next to him. "How was your first night?"

"It was great," I spilled, wanting to process my experience from the night before. "I felt so... peaceful. I don't think I've ever slept so well."

Trent smiled a huge smile. "This is a pretty great place. I'm so glad my family lives near this church."

"They do?" I was intrigued.

"Yeah. Tyrell and I both. We've known each other and gone to church here for years."

"We should hang out more," Tyrell suggested. "Welcome to the church."

I glowed with warmth at that. I'd spent my whole life looking for a second family, envying my brother's ability to go have barbeques with his dad and siblings. Now, it seemed I suddenly had several families even beyond those of my mom and dad.

More with each passing moment, I began to feel like I had another church family. I now had a new home.

After the retreat, I participated in the church's youth group as often as I could. Every Friday night was youth night. We'd praise and worship just like we had at the retreat, and then the youth pastor would talk to us about a Biblical topic and how we could apply it in our lives.

It was at one of these youth nights that I noticed Jordan for the first time. He was running around the church like a ninja with a camera, ducking between people and squatting to get the perfect angle on the evening's speaker.

I'd seen him before, standing in the media booth at the back of the church. He was just about my age, but he seemed to be responsible for helping to record each service and lecture the church hosted.

On this evening, he knelt by me, getting down on one knee in the aisle while everyone else was sitting and listening intently. He seemed focused on getting the perfect shot of the man who was speaking.

"Romans Ten tells us," the speaker was saying, "that if you confess with your mouth that Jesus is Lord, if you believe in your heart that God raised him from the dead, then you will be saved. You then become a new creation. For it is with your heart that you believe and are justified, and it is with your mouth that you confess and are saved. You are then free to seek out your identity in Christ."

Seek out your identity.

That sounded like what I had been looking for all these years. Who was I, really? I'd thought that meeting my father would help with that—and it had, in some ways. But I still felt a little empty inside. I still felt like I didn't know who I was, or why I was here.

"When we accept Jesus as our Lord and savior," the speaker continued, "then we become part of his mission. Can anyone tell me what that mission is?"

A girl in the front row raised her hand. "To win souls to Christ!"

"Very good," the speaker nodded approvingly. "Jesus' mission is to save the lost. He died because he loves us. Jesus is proof that God would do anything for us. And it's our task to love creation, just as He does. In Christ, we will find the true purpose for which He placed us on this Earth."

Our identity is found in Christ.

That just felt right to me. It felt like the answer I'd been searching for.

I couldn't help but glance at the boy with the camera as he sprang to his feet and moved again, sliding around the edges of the church to capture a new angle. I'd seen the finished recordings of talks and church services, and they were impressive. Was this boy behind all of that?

At the end of the youth nights, snacks were

served. We'd spend time socializing around the table stocked with coke and fruit and cookies, talking and thinking over what we'd just heard. It was good to have that kind of fellowship, and I often felt hungry after hearing such profound words.

This evening I stood with Trent and Tyrell, as usual. I'd been adopted as something of a little sister to their whole group of friends, and I loved the friendship and accountability they gave me. But tonight, someone new joined the circle. The camera boy sidled in, looking around our group with a curious expression.

"I'm Jordan," he said, reaching out to shake my hand. Tyrell made friendly small talk with him. But Jordan's eyes kept straying to me.

The attention felt good. I wasn't used to anyone going out of their way to be near me.

At the end of the night, as Trent and Tyrell packed up to go home, Jordan hung back with me.

"I'm not sure I got your name," he said.

"Chikiya." I held my hand out, and he shook it.

"Well, it's great to meet you, Chikiya. I don't know how I've never noticed you before. When did you start coming here?"

"Just a few months ago." I smiled, blushing pleasantly. "Would you like to hang out sometime?"

"Yeah," Jordan said with a big smile. "Yeah. I'd like that."

CHAPTER 8

Jordan and I talked on the phone every day for months. He seemed interested in everything about me. What were my plans for my life? What did I think of the last sermon? What did I do for fun?

I learned that he was an aspiring cameraman who had been going to the church for many years. He was an essential part of its media team, which was mostly young people due to the rapidly changing technology of the 2010s. I was impressed by his work.

His interest in me felt validating. Here was

someone who played an important role in the church, and he wanted to get to know me. In some ways, I felt like I had finally arrived as part of the church community. Here was a church friend who knew me not as "the new girl," but simply as Chikiya. And he wanted to get to know me better.

Jordan was very sweet and complimentary when we talked. He'd compliment my eyes, my smile, my personality. He found my laugh beautiful and appreciated my enthusiasm. Better yet, he was a church boy. That meant he believed the same thing about morals and accountability as I did—or so I thought.

Perhaps I should have known that he had romance on his mind early on. When he asked me to be his girlfriend after two months of speaking nearly every day, I was not surprised.

For our first date, we got on the metro train with no plan for where we'd end up. Neither of us had a car, so we rode until we got to what seemed like an appealing stop, then stepped out to survey the land. A big, bright McDonald's sign blinked at us from across the street.

"Want to go there?" Jordan asked.

I smiled shyly. "Okay."

As the months passed, our relationship escalated into hand-holding and timid kisses. I wasn't too sure about my feelings. This was my first real relationship. It felt new and exciting, and scary all at once. Was I doing it right? Was *he* doing it right? Did I want to marry him?

The answer to that last question, I eventually discerned, was "no." But I loved his kindness and attention, and the romance of being with a boy from church. And I didn't want to stop dating him just because I didn't want to marry him. If I didn't date before marriage, how was I supposed to learn who I was in a relationship, or what relationships could be like?

For about two months, our relationship was like

a dream. I wasn't madly in love, but I liked so many things about Jordan's sweet, quiet manner, his skill with the camera, and his apparent godliness. Wasn't this what first love was supposed to be? Finding someone you were compatible with and exploring romance together?

But then, things took a turn for the strange.

We'd been dating for about two months when a girl I'd never seen before began showing up to church functions. Her name was Amanda, and although I didn't know who she was, she seemed to have it out for me.

I'd catch her staring at me, often with a scowl on her face, when I noticed her at church events. When I saw her talking to a group of my churchmates one evening, I decided to try to investigate.

I sidled up to the group, wanting to listen and hear more before I spoke up.

"I'm Amanda," I heard her introduce herself

to one of the boys in the group. She extended a manicured hand for him to shake, and everything about the movement was flirtatious.

This 'Amanda' was undeniably pretty, but something about her came off as a little *wrong*. Every move she made felt exaggerated, like she was performing. Why and for what audience, I didn't know.

"Hi," I inserted myself in the conversation loud enough to be heard, but didn't let on that I knew what she'd said. "I'm Chikiya." I thrust my own hand toward her to be shaken, but she drew back, looking dismayed. Or disgusted.

"Oh," she said. "Chikiya. I've heard about you."

Then she turned and left the group, leaving all of us baffled.

"What was that about?" Tyrell asked, peering at me with concern. I could feel his protective older brother instinct kicking in, wondering what I wasn't telling him.

The problem was, I didn't know either. "I don't know," I said honestly, as I watched Amanda leave. "I've never seen her before in my life."

As the weeks wore on, the situation with Amanda grew stranger. Jordan seemed not to notice this new girl in church who had it out for me, and I avoided the subject with him because I didn't like to think about her rude behavior. She seemed to have just come from nowhere, determined to spread false rumors about me.

I remembered being jumped when I first moved into my father's neighborhood, so I thought perhaps this sort of thing just happened sometimes. Sometimes one person just decided to make life difficult for another, for no clear reason.

It was one of Jordan's friends who finally told

me the truth. At church one day, I was venting to Trent and Tyrell about the rumors this girl kept starting, and my inability to get her to leave me alone. The boy who handled the sound in the church media booth was packing up his equipment nearby, and he overheard.

"Oh, Amanda?" he asked. "She's Jordan's ex-girlfriend. She's crazy."

That sentence froze me like ice. Jordan's ex-girlfriend? He'd never mentioned her to me. Was he really so unaware of what was going on that he didn't notice that his ex had invaded the church youth group, with the seeming sole mission of tarnishing my reputation?

"She's been saying that you started it," he continued. "That you won't leave her alone."

That was the last straw. I knew that confronting Amanda would be playing into her hands. She *wanted* me to lose my cool and appear to be the "bad guy" in front of everyone.

But Jordan. Jordan had to know something about this. I had to talk to him immediately.

I pulled out my phone and began to text him.

"Jordan, can we talk?"

"Sure, baby. What about?"

"Your ex-girlfriend is here. She's trying to mess things up for me."

"Amanda? Oh, I'm so sorry, baby. I've told her a thousand times that it's over between us, but she just won't let me go."

Somehow, Jordan's reassurance that he had tried to cut her loose and could do nothing about her behavior didn't fully soothe my worries. What kind of woman went so far out of her way to trash talk someone?

Then the messages started.

I logged onto Facebook one day to see the

message from an account with Amanda's picture on it:

Boyfriend-stealer.

I stared at the message, wondering what I had done to earn this.

He's not your boyfriend, I typed back. _He's with me now._

Liar. The word hit me hard. I took my honesty very seriously. Then: _I'm pregnant with his baby._

I sat back in my chair at that, my heart pounding.

Amanda had been spreading false rumors about me since the first time I lay eyes on her. She had never told the truth. But could I be sure she wasn't telling the truth about _this_? It seemed such a bold, crazy thing to lie about.

I knew I had to talk to Jordan again, to get to the bottom of it.

Anxiety boiled in my gut as I watched Jordan walk into the restaurant and look around for me. I'd planned things this way for a reason: we were in public, in a nice place with a good reputation. Surely he'd be honest with me here. Surely he couldn't get too upset with me for asking him about Amanda's seemingly ludicrous claim.

My heart pounded as Jordan saw me and smiled. He slid into the seat across from me, as cool and relaxed as anything. He reached his hands across the table to hold mine.

"It's good to see you, baby."

My mouth was dry when I opened it. I knew I couldn't wait any longer.

"Jordan," I blurted out, "are you having sex with Amanda?"

He recoiled as though I'd hit him. "What? No! Is she saying that I did?"

"She's saying that she's pregnant with your baby."

Jordan let his head sink into his hands, a movement of exasperation and despair. "Of course she is. Of course she would. Baby, I am so sorry. I promise you there is no way that could be possible."

Relief flooded through me. Jordan seemed so genuinely distressed and surprised by this news. If he said he wasn't sleeping with Amanda, it was good enough for me.

In hindsight, it's clear to me now how toxic this relationship was. Jordan was treating me, and maybe other women, in ways that weren't good for me. But because I felt like I was in love, I tolerated it. I told myself that everything had to be alright.

Then, things got even stranger.

I was at home late one night, doing homework, when my phone rang. I glanced at the caller ID and frowned. I didn't know this number, and these were the days when spam calls were still rare.

I picked up the phone hesitantly. "Hello?"

On the other end, a girl was crying. "Chikiya?" I recognized Amanda's voice, broken though it was.

She talked to me about how much she loved Jordan, and how I had taken him from her. She tried to manipulate me, saying it was my fault that he had broken up with her.

Then, she dropped the bomb.

"If I can't get back with Jordan, I'm going to kill myself."

Adrenaline shot through me, sending my heart into my throat. "What? No! No, don't do that! Stay on the line with me. Please? We'll get you some help."

I scrambled to the computer and began to look up suicide hotline numbers. While I kept her talking, Amanda poured out feelings that seemed genuine.

"I just love Jordan so much," she said tearfully. "I can't believe he's sleeping with another woman."

I *wasn't* sleeping with him, but that hardly seemed worth pointing out as she was sobbing. "I need him, Chikiya. Break up with him."

Something occurred to me suddenly.

"How did you get this number?"

Silence on the other end of the line. But I already knew the answer.

She got it out of Jordan's phone. It was the only way. No one Amanda knew had my number except for Trent, Tyrell, and Jordan. And I knew that my church big brothers would never give it to her.

Jordan probably wouldn't have, either. That meant she'd had access to his phone. He'd left her alone with it, at some point.

My pulse was beginning to slow down, an awful certainty replacing my terror.

This call wasn't a cry for help, was it? It was an escalation of her attempts to get me to leave Jordan.

Who she saw as her own. Maybe because *he* had told her that.

But the suicide hotline number had loaded on my computer screen by then, and I wasn't taking any chances.

"Amanda? Stay on the line. I'm going to put you on three-way."

But by the time the suicide hotline operator picked up the phone, Amanda had hung up.

Jordan's defenses were less ready when I confronted him again. By now he'd bought a car, which he used to drive to his job—and to drive me to school, sometimes.

I told him, as we sat in the school parking lot one morning, about Amanda's phone call.

He looked at his hands in his lap. He seemed to

know he couldn't deny the implications.

"Yeah," he said finally. "Yeah, I saw her. She called me, all crazy and desperate like that. Said she had to see me, or she was going to do something awful. I went to the bathroom. She must have gotten my phone then."

He glanced up at me. "It's true, you know. What I told you before. She's lying about having my baby. She just wants me all for herself."

"And did you tell her you were hers?" I hated the taste of the words on my tongue. I hated doubting Jordan, questioning him. But his ex(?)-girlfriend was making my life hell, and I deserved answers.

"Maybe I wasn't... as clear with her as I could have been. But I'm just yours now, baby. I promise."

After that, I was consumed with a horrible doubt and fear. Amanda's behavior just didn't add up. She was manipulative, sure. But did I really believe she would still be behaving this way, months after Jordan had cut her off?

Or was something else going on? Was he still telling her he loved her?

And if her, then who else?

Seized by suspicion, I took a page from Amanda's book. The next time Jordan and I were together and he left to use the restroom, I grabbed his phone and rifled through his texts.

"Jordan??? I need to talk to you!" That was a text from Amanda, timestamped to that same day.

"I love you baby. Call me." That one was from a contact named Kelli.

I opened the conversation with Kelli, my heart pounding. What I saw filled me with rage.

"Do you have a girlfriend?" One of Kelli's earlier texts read, clearly testing the waters.

"Nah, baby. I'm single. How about you?"

"Well, there was a boy, but I just broke up with him."

I set the phone down, feeling cold. I now knew the truth: that Jordan had never been only mine, and I suspected he hadn't been honest with these women either.

When Jordan returned, I had trouble looking at him. Finally, I let my findings burst out of me.

"You've been texting Amanda... and this Kelli person? And how many others, Jordan? How many other women?"

I shouldn't have accepted his apologies. I shouldn't have believed his reassurances. At some level, I already understood that we were going nowhere fast.

But he had been so *sweet*. He was the first boy who had shown romantic interest in me. He was a church boy, for crying out loud! At the time, I assumed that people I met through church would try just as hard to love and honor God and keep his commandments as I did. How could someone who attended youth nights just like I did lie and cheat without remorse?

It seemed unbelievable. So I decided not to believe it. For a while.

CHAPTER 9

After that conversation with Jordan, Amanda disappeared entirely. She stopped coming to youth group, stopped messaging and calling me. So when Jordan told me he had broken up with her once and for all—in order to be with just me—I believed him.

But not all of the changes were for the better.

I was approaching my high school graduation. Jordan had graduated two years earlier. We had been dating for about six months now, and we stood on the cusp of summer and of our new lives as adults.

I planned to attend the local community college to get as many class credits as I could affordably, then transfer later to a school with a highly rated criminal justice program. I knew that Jordan hadn't attended college and didn't plan to, but I assumed he had a plan for his career.

But it seemed that *one* part of his plan for the future was clear. Almost as soon as Amanda disappeared, Jordan began pressing me about sex and marriage.

"I want to marry you, baby," he'd say, leaning over the steering wheel of his car and grinning goofily at me. "You're the one."

A year earlier, that might have made me happy. But now, it made my skin crawl. Something felt *wrong* about it. He'd been *at least* flirting with two other women until last month, and now he wanted to marry me?

He'd lay his hand on my thigh, and his intentions

would become clear. "But... don't you think we ought to try it first?" he'd venture.

I'd scramble out of the passenger seat when he pulled up to the curve. "Jordan, I'm not having sex with you. You know I want to wait until marriage before opening that door. We go to the same church, for crying out loud!"

"Sure, the Bible says no sex until you meet your husband. But what if I'm your husband, and I'm just impatient to get started?"

I was so deep in the relationship by now that I didn't realize how wrong this was. He had eased me into it over the course of nearly a year. First it was his kindness, his flattery, his interest in my life. Then a few months of good, chaste dating where I thought I was his one and only.

Now, of course, I knew that that had never been true. He'd had other girls on the side. Or was *I* his side girl the whole time?

Soon, the text messages started.

Chikiya, I want to talk about this 'sex' thing.

Chikiya, I have needs!

When are you going to give it up? We both know it's what we want.

If you won't have sex with me Chikiya, then I'm going to have sex with someone else.

If this was what having all of Jordan's attention meant, I didn't like it. He may have broken up with Amanda once and for all in order to keep me, but now he seemed to expect me to fill her shoes. And with Jordan's recent demands, Amanda's story that she'd been pregnant with his child began to seem much more plausible.

To make matters worse, he seemed to have opinions about every aspect of my life now. He had ideas about how I should spend my time. He wanted to know where I was constantly when I wasn't with him.

He said it was just because he loved me and he

didn't want me to get hurt, but I knew that wasn't true. If this was how he showed his love, where had this behavior been for the first six months we were together?

I avoided Jordan as much as I could, but somehow I never thought about breaking up with him. Jordan and I were together. We had been for so long that that felt like just "the way things were." And somewhere, maybe, I held out hope that his behavior would get better.

He had been so good to me once upon a time, after all. And he *did* seem to have put the other girls aside.

My high school graduating party was excruciatingly awkward.

I was resplendent in my black robe with the blue, gold, and white tassels of my high school. I felt so accomplished and so excited for my next step that nothing could bring me down.

But Jordan came to the party, and my family's

distaste for him was palpable. You could feel it in the air.

I'm not sure what they saw that I didn't. I hadn't confided about our relationship troubles with anyone except my stepmom, Wanda, who promised to keep them to herself. She had told me simply, "You need to make a choice," as Jordan's behavior toward me became more and more demanding.

Still, my father seemed to sense that something was wrong. So did my mother, who had come up to visit for the party.

Jordan moved around the open house, circulating, talking to people, smiling and laughing like nothing was wrong. He smiled at *me* like nothing was wrong. But I couldn't bring myself to return his smile. I'd have to look away from him and smile at someone else.

My dad's mother had moved in with us a few months earlier. She was a genuine woman with a big smile and a big heart. But when she saw Jordan, her smile shut right down. I saw her eyes dart from him to me, saw her brow furrow.

What was so obvious about him that I was missing? Had I simply become blind to his behavior by being exposed to it for so long?

The following week, Jordan dropped me off to work at my summer job. This was routine, assumed: of course I would get my ride from Jordan. We had argued about my refusal to have sex with him earlier, but that was nothing new.

But something felt *wrong* from the moment I got into the car. One of his friends was in the back seat. That wasn't a first in itself, but this friend seemed sullen and serious. As we drove, I started to wonder *why* he was there. Where was Jordan dropping *him* off?

As Jordan navigated the city traffic, he didn't say a word. I could feel the pressure of the text messages from the previous nights weighing down on me. It wasn't hard to guess what he was thinking when he refused to speak with me now. He had one thing on his mind.

The hair on the back of my neck stood up. I could feel his friend's eyes on me in the back of the car. His friend said nothing, but that in itself spoke volumes. He had known that this was coming, and he was there to take Jordan's side.

When we finally pulled up to my workplace, Jordan grabbed my arm and physically shoved me out of the car.

I stomped onto the curb and into my workplace, shaking.

I never looked back at his car.

When my shift at work ended, Jordan arrived to pick me up. My stomach churned when I saw him. I had half-expected him not to show.

But he did show up, and he shoved the car door open for me. He didn't look at me as I sat down in the passenger seat. The tension in the car was so thick, it was hard to breathe.

What had happened to the boy who had once impressed me by being so kind and sweet? Why was he treating me like this?

When we pulled up in front of my parents' house, he got out of the driver's seat and stormed around to the back seat of his car. That was where I'd slung my backpack and a few other items that I'd made a habit of leaving in his car over the months he'd been driving me to work.

One by one, he began pulling these items out and throwing them violently onto the curb. A stream of names I didn't even want to think about came from his lips, directed at me. He left me on the curb with my heart hammering in my chest, adrenaline surging through me.

I won't share with you what he called me here, but his anger at me denying him sex was clear.

The angry, reckless text messages continued. I deleted his number from my phone, determined to ignore him.

As far as I was concerned, our relationship was over. There was no 'goodbye.' He didn't get to treat me like this and still deserve a goodbye or an explanation.

He approached me the following Sunday at church, all repentant pleas for forgiveness, but I ignored him. Having Trent and Tyrell there helped. I'd told them everything, too, and they stared menacingly over my shoulder while I pointedly ignored his pleas.

In time, I felt I could breathe easier. I even still missed Jordan sometimes—his good side. The side he'd shown me when I wasn't his only girl. I missed our talks and his laughter, and how special he made me feel.

But the relief was much greater than the sadness.

This had been the first romance of my life, and only as time passed did I begin to understand how messed up it was.

"That isn't *normal*, Chikiya," Tyrell told me one night, distress written all over his face as I poured out the time Amanda called me threatening suicide. "No one should have to live with that."

Trent smacked himself on the forehead. "I should have known something was wrong. I should have known as soon as she showed up. I've never *seen* anybody act like that before. I should have known he was playing you both."

My big brothers' validations helped me begin to feel solid again. Helped me to feel sure of myself.

I had a lot of healing to do. I'm not sure I understood then just how much. But I did know one thing.

I was about to start college, and that meant a whole new world lay ahead of me.

CHAPTER 10

The beginning of my college career was a time of transition. The plan was for me to continue to live with Wanda, but the makeup of the family was changing. My father was to be deployed for three long years in California, and my grandmother had made the decision to move out on her own. She didn't tell any of us *why*, at first, but I'd learn later.

That left just Wanda and me, sharing a house while I attended the local community college. I certainly didn't mind. We got along well and we went to the same church. But it was *strange* to share a house with just one other woman as a new adult myself. It was the closest I'd ever come to living alone.

My plan for college was simple: I'd get as many transferable credits at community college rates as I could, then transfer to my target school to complete the more specialized coursework that a Criminal Justice degree would require.

My target school? Bowie State. The historically Black college was a place I knew I'd feel at home, and it was close enough to home that I could stay with my stepmother for the duration of my undergraduate career.

At community college, I learned to sharpen my skills for success. College challenged me academically in ways that high school hadn't, and I had to learn how to set goals and accomplish them.

As simple as this might sound, it wasn't simple in practice. As my coursework grew more difficult, so did the plans I'd have to make. Setting a goal and accomplishing it was no longer as simple as just completing an assignment on time. Now I had to strategize when I would do research, when I would spend time in memorization, and what steps I would need to take to successfully perform at my best.

My hard work paid off. By halfway through my first semester, I was one of the top-performing students in several of my community college classes. This led a classmate, Brenda, to ask me for help with the writing class we both shared. Happy to be able to help, I agreed to read her papers and give her feedback.

That was how I met Andy.

Andy was Brenda's brother. He was the only boy in a family of five, surrounded by four sisters. Maybe that's why he was so comfortable talking to me. We first met when he showed up in the background of a Facetime conversation that Brenda and I were having about our schoolwork, and the conversation just flowed. Before I knew it, he was asking for my number. I gave it to him.

Andy was already attending Bowie State. He'd sometimes drive me up there to get to know the campus on weekends. We were also both fierce football fans, and having him around to watch games with soothed my soul in my dad's absence.

From the start, I struggled with my feelings for Andy. I *wanted* to be able to like and trust another man, but my experience with Jordan had scarred me deeply. How did I know that Andy wasn't going to turn controlling and start pressuring me to have sex? How did I know there wasn't something he was hiding from me?

But Andy seemed easygoing. I almost didn't notice that I was drifting away from my church community during this time. Between the intense amount of studying and schoolwork I was doing and the visits to Bowie State's campus, I was barely making it to church on Sundays.

That Jordan was present at the church services and youth nights didn't help. I ignored his attempts to get my attention, but I was no longer as comfortable there as I'd once been.

Slowly but surely, Andy's combination of casual ease and unapologetic stubbornness began to charm me. By the time I received my acceptance letter to Bowie State, we were more than friends. For the second time in my life, I was going steady with a man.

Community college prepared me for the big leagues academically. But nothing could have prepared me for the social challenges I'd encounter at Bowie State.

Everyone who's been to college straight out of high school knows the buzz that comes with that new feeling of adulthood. For me, community college still felt a lot like high school. But Bowie State was different. The college campus was its own community, run and populated mostly by young adults.

For the first time in our young lives, no one could *really* tell us what to do. Most of the students at Bowie paid their own rent, and many were even old enough to drink. This led to a lot of parties.

I avoided the wild parties. Like all colleges, Bowie State had its party houses and its more mature communities, where people met for business networking and fellowship. Andy and I went to the more mellow parties together, spending time with his classmates and friends over pizza and good music.

Andy wasn't a churchgoing person, but he was a good man. In his long silences and furtive glances, I'd sometimes imagine I saw him thinking about our future together, too.

And there was one thing that my college classmates agreed on that my churchmates didn't. According to them, I couldn't expect someone to marry me without having sex with me first. So as my comfort with Andy grew, I began to consider the possibility.

We were both virgins. Neither of us had ever experienced sex before. Andy was open with me about that, and that made me feel better. We were both looking to experience it—in part because our college peers made us feel like we had to.

And so, one night at his father's house, Andy and I crossed that bridge together. After that, I felt closer to him than I'd ever felt before.

However, this started to change after I noticed something that bothered me. Andy was receiving messages from another woman. A lot of them.

I couldn't see her face on his Facebook wall or see her texts pop up on his phone without feeling certain that she wanted to be more than just friends.

As time passed, Andy and I began to argue. I now realize that we were moving in two different directions. I wasn't comfortable with his closeness with his ex-girlfriend, Kathryn, and I wasn't sure I wanted to be with him forever. Andy wanted our relationship to be long-term, but he refused to cut contact with his ex-girlfriend for me.

In hindsight, our fights became toxic. We were attracted to each other, but also constantly trying to change each other. Andy tried to convince me that his Kathryn wasn't interested in him that way and that he had eyes only for me, while I grew suspicious and felt he didn't respect my need for security after what had happened with Jordan. We became almost addicted to the conflict.

Things came to a head one day when he left me alone in his car while picking up food at a restaurant. His phone lay abandoned on the dashboard, and I stared at it with my heart pounding in my chest. I remembered too well what had happened with Jordan's phone, and what I'd discovered when I went through his messages. Just like with Jordan, Andy and I knew each other's smartphone PIN codes.

With a trembling hand, I reached out and picked Andy's phone up.

I entered the PIN, and was treated to a notification. He had half a dozen unread text messages—and all of them were from Kathryn.

There was nothing sexual or romantic in the texts. But there was affection, and that looked a lot to me like flirting. They clearly talked about everything together—including about me. The blood drained from my face as I saw Andy explaining to his ex that I wasn't comfortable with her, and that he'd done his best to allay my fears.

I don't claim to be the good guy here. I like to think I've grown since this time, both in clearly defining my own boundaries and in respecting other people's. I hadn't yet realized that I just wasn't in an emotional place where I could date a man who was best friends with his ex. And Andy hadn't realized just how deep my scars were, or that he couldn't expect my needs on that matter to change.

All I knew at the time was that I couldn't tolerate Andy's conversations with this woman. The thought of them talking, her smiling and batting her eyelashes at him, made me break out in a cold sweat. And he clearly wanted to keep me around, but he didn't want to have to do what I asked on this matter. He thought he could change my mind.

When Andy got back to the car, I exploded at him.

"I asked you not to talk to her anymore." I shoved the phone in his face with tears in my eyes. "And you talked to her about *me*. How could you?"

The hurt and anger were clear on Andy's face. He took my lack of trust in him as a betrayal. "Chikiya," he shot back, "I am *not* losing my best friend over this."

Hearing him call *her* his best friend hurt even more. I shielded my face with my hand to hide my tears.

Andy drove me home in silence. I thought we'd get over this fight, just like we'd gotten over so many others.

I didn't know it yet, but that was the beginning of the end.

CHAPTER 11

I stepped into my parents' house to find it silent. This puzzled me. Normally my stepmom would be watching TV, talking on the phone, or noisily cooking in the kitchen. The house wasn't empty and the lights were on. But something wasn't right.

I was standing in the living room, glancing through all the doors in hopes of catching sight of Wanda, when she came walking out of the kitchen slowly. I could see by the way she looked at me that something had disturbed her.

"Chikiya, sit down," she said, guiding me to the living room sofa. "There's something I have to tell you. About your grandmother."

For the second time that day, my heart started hammering in my chest. My grandmother had seemed to be in good health when she lived with us, but she was an older woman. What could have happened to her?

"Chikiya, your grandmother—she's passed away."

The words hit me like a ton of bricks. My mouth fell open.

"She had…" Wanda raised a hand to cover her mouth, tearing up. "She had stomach cancer," she managed. "She didn't tell any of us because—because she didn't want us to worry."

I sat back heavily on the couch, staring into space. "That's why she moved out," I said faintly. "She didn't want us to know she was sick."

"It looks that way," Wanda half-whispered. "And I guess she wanted to get to know you before she went."

My heart sank. I remembered my grandmother as a beautiful, vibrant presence in my life. She had always been there with a genuine smile and a little joke to at least try to make me laugh. She had always seemed interested in everybody, and she seemed to feel things very deeply. I guess she didn't want to feel our hurt over her sickness.

"Does granddad know?" I whispered. My dad's parents had lived a thousand miles apart for many years, and I had only spoken to him on the phone. He had never come to visit while she lived with us, and I somehow doubted she had let him in on her secret.

"I just got done telling him," Wanda said, and she suddenly looked weary. "He's having a hard time with it."

At that moment, I felt something inside me

shift. I had always been a child in this family. The one who was taken care *of.* But I was a young adult now. I was in college. And suddenly, it seemed like my stepmom could use a caregiver herself.

"Why don't you go lay down, Wanda?" I stood up. "I'm gonna make you some tea."

I hadn't been to church much at all since I'd started attending Bowie State. But this Sunday, Wanda and I went together and sat in silence, grieving for the woman we had both known and loved. I stared into space, still not quite believing it myself.

During the sermon, the pastor spoke about hope. I was able to cry a little. I was able to heal a little.

Little did I know, this was only the beginning of a string of losses.

The next time I got into Andy's car, there was silence between us. I wasn't sure what to say. I almost felt guilty about what I'd said to him last time—almost. But I was still too hurt and angry that he didn't seem to care how I felt about his conversations with his ex. I think both of us still thought that we could stay together if we could only change the other person.

"Chikiya," he said, "I won't apologize for talking to Kathryn. But I will say I'm sorry for how it makes you feel. I never want you to be upset like that, Chikiya. I just don't know how to make you feel better."

I couldn't have this argument. Not right now. With my grandmother gone and my father out of the house, it felt like the world was closing in around me. I longed for the easy warmth and affection that

Andy and I had once shared, and the way I'd felt less lonely when he was around. I wanted to forget about everything but that.

"Andy, my grandmother died." It came out of my mouth, just like that. I was still staring ahead a little, still not really processing what had happened.

"Oh. Oh, Chikiya."

And for a moment, it seemed like our troubles were forgotten. Andy pulled me into his arms and held me tight while I cried into his shoulder.

The few weeks that followed seemed like a very short time. While I gradually adjusted to the new normal—to the knowledge that my grandma would never walk through the door again—I was still emotionally fragile when I woke up to find Wanda sitting on the edge of my bed.

My heart started pounding in my chest as soon

as I saw her. She'd never done this before. It had to mean something was wrong.

"Chikiya," she said, very softly, "I'm sorry to wake you. It's your granddad. He passed away in the night. I thought you should know."

I rolled over in my bed and buried my face in my pillow. The bright light streaming in through the curtains felt cold where it fell across my bed. How did the sun dare to shine on a day like this? I'd never met my grandfather face-to-face, and now I was never going to.

I sobbed into my pillow for a long time. I cried so long that I missed Andy when he came to pick me up for school.

With both of my grandparents gone, it almost felt like there was no point in trying to heal the wound that had opened up in my heart. Was I going to lose somebody else, just when I got used to the idea of never seeing my grandparents again? With my mom and my father both in another state, anything seemed possible. Only Wanda seemed real to me. She was the only one who I felt sure I'd see again.

I'm sure this impacted the way I was with Andy. While I'd clung to him for comfort at first, this second death had shaken me. I was no longer sure I wanted to reach out for help with my grief. After all, the way we move through grief is to feel it and experience it. My close contacts with Andy were helping me do that.

But right now, I wasn't sure I wanted to open up. I wasn't sure I wanted to feel anything at all. And I continued to be troubled by his relationship with his best friend—another woman, who I feared might steal him away. We continued to argue about that, even as I grieved.

I think that Andy saw that I was fading. I think he was afraid of his behavior hurting me again. I think he was afraid that he wasn't willing to do what I wanted—to change one of the most important relationships in his life. I think that's why I got a string of texts from him, just days after my grandfather died:

I think we both know I'm not what you need.

I'm tired of all the fighting.

Our relationship is toxic.

I wish you all the best.

Goodbye.

It was official. I was alone.

Without Andy around, I started driving myself to school. I started keeping to myself, largely isolating myself from my church friends and family.

My default state was a kind of numbness. I didn't want to feel anything, so I just went through the motions each day. Sometimes I'd wake up at night, haunted by a terrible sense of loss and loneliness. Remembering all the people in my life who weren't coming back.

For the first time, I started to understand the allure of drinking. The people who I saw drunk at parties at school didn't seem to have a care in the world. When I began to grow more careless with my own alcohol intake, I soon found that I felt warm and fuzzy. For a while, I seemed to be able to forget my problems.

My old sense of caution was gone. When the real world seemed so bleak and lonely, escaping into the world of partying and drinking had more and more appeal. Deep down, I knew I was going down a dangerous road, but I didn't think my church friends would understand or help me.

Be careful, Chikiya, a little voice whispered in my head when I picked up my first bottle. I was living in my own way, largely ignoring what I'd learned in church. So I thought it couldn't be God—why would He reach out to me when I was no longer seeking Him out?

Be careful of what? I wondered when I heard that voice. *It's not like things can get any worse.*

Drinking wasn't the only way I sought solace, either. I'd always known that men were interested in my body, and before I'd viewed this as a danger. I didn't want to get into a relationship with someone who only wanted me for sex. But now, that started to seem appealing. Sex could give me a temporary companion, a temporary warmth. I wouldn't have to open up to anyone, or get close enough to miss them when they disappeared, if I stuck to casual sex.

Be careful, Chikiya, the voice whispered again, this time louder, before I followed the first man into his bedroom. But I thought about how scared and lonely I felt when I woke up in the middle of the night. I just wanted to be close to someone. Just for a little while.

Sex reminded me of Andy. It reminded me of what I had once hoped to someday have with Jordan. It seemed like a preview of the life I'd hoped to have. If I couldn't have a loving, stable relationship with a man who would marry me, I could at least have part of it.

As you can probably guess, I was going nowhere fast. My relationship with God at this time was nonexistent. I sometimes doubted if He was even there. My church had failed to protect me from this loss and pain, so why should I go back there?

My grades dropped below the standard I held for myself. What relationships I had left suffered. I spoke less and less to Wanda. I spoke to almost nobody at all. I withdrew into myself, and *from* myself. I didn't even want *me* to know what I was thinking.

During this time, there were a few friends who tried to keep the lines of communication open. But they didn't go about doing it in the best way.

I'd known Linda since Andy and I were dating. We'd met while she was working at a store near my parents' house, and we'd immediately clicked. It turned out that we lived only a block or two away from each other, and we both attended Bowie State.

Soon Linda had become my best female friend. She was a girl with a big heart, a big smile, and a strong sense of fun.

As the school year progressed, two other girls had joined our circle. Tisha was a classmate who began studying with Linda and me, and the three of us met Rachel at the punch bowl at a homecoming dance.

There's a verse in the Bible that says:

"Do not be deceived; bad company corrupts good character."

—1 Corinthians 15:33

I was about to learn that that was true.

For a long time, it seemed like these girls had my back. I felt I could talk to Linda about anything, but she didn't push or pry when I stopped talking to *anyone* because I didn't want to process my own feelings. Rachel always seemed to be up for a good time—by which I mean she took me to more and more parties, with more and more alcohol.

But it soon became clear that there was something wrong with our clique. My grief and my withdrawal exposed cracks that had always been there in our friendships.

Rachel took me to all the parties I wanted, but she soon began to ask questions and demand answers of me. What was I thinking when I sat there, so silent? What was it that I wasn't telling her? There was obviously *something*. It was a man, wasn't it? A man I didn't want to tell her about. Didn't she have a right to know?

The girls began to talk behind my back. They began to judge my words and actions, and my insecurity reared its head. I would try to change myself to fit in with them—but in the process would only find myself feeling emptier and less accepted.

They claimed that I had changed—that I wasn't the same person they'd first come to know. That I didn't share with them the way they wanted me to.

That I didn't belong with them anymore.

I just wanted to be numb. I wanted to forget. But it soon became clear that for Rachel, nothing would ever be enough.

She thought that if I was her friend, I should tell her everything. Anything in my life that she learned about without me being the first to tell her, she took as an insult and a threat. For my part, I just didn't feel like opening up to anyone right now. I was dealing with a lot, and talking about it with people who judged me felt like it would just make matters worse.

In her mind, this made me the bad guy. By keeping my silence and withdrawing socially, in her mind, I was breaking the group's trust. I had set myself apart from them. I was acting like I was better than them.

I found all this ludicrous. My grief was my own. It had nothing to do with these other women. It *certainly* didn't have to do with any sense of superiority.

But Rachel talked more than I did, and so she became the storyteller. She told Linda and Tisha that I was looking down on *all* of them. That I didn't trust them. That I wasn't interested in being friends anymore. I became the topic of their conversations, rather than a part of their group.

"Oh, look," Rachel said with a disgusted sneer as I approached the girls' table in the cafeteria one day. "Look who decided to grace us with her presence."

I glared hostilely at Rachel. Then I noticed that the other girls were watching me.

"Chikiya…" Linda said carefully, but Tischa cut her off.

"Cut the crap, Chikiya. What aren't you telling us? You never talk to us about anything *important* these days. We don't know what you're doing. What *are* you doing?"

I kept my mouth shut. There was no way I was going to open up to these girls about my loss, my grief, my loneliness. Not when they were acting like *this*.

"See?" Rachel insisted. "She thinks she's too good for us. I don't know why we hang around with her at all."

The words hurt, but I didn't want them to see that. Even I was surprised by just how *much* they hurt.

Linda was looking at me uncertainly. "Chikiya? Do you have anything you want to say to that?"

I didn't know what to say. Was any of what Rachel said true?

I didn't look down on my friends. I didn't distrust them—not exactly. But did I really want to be friends the way we once had been? Did I really want to open up to them about my grief and fear?

Did I want to open up to anyone, if it meant I might start feeling things again?

Soon, the decision was made for me. My words seemed frozen in my mouth, unable to come out, as

Rachel planted seeds of suspicion in the other girls' hearts and nurtured them with daily whispers.

I didn't have the words to tell Linda what was going on, and I wasn't sure I wanted to. After everything that had happened in the last few years, I had difficulty trusting people.

But at the same time, I loved Linda. I felt like I was losing my best friend. Wasn't there anything I could do to keep her?

Rachel had been proven right about one thing. I *was* sleeping with a man I hadn't told them about. Was there any point in explaining that she was wrong about the rest, but that I just really didn't want to talk right now?

"I don't know what's come over you, Chikiya," Linda told me one day, her beautiful eyebrows furrowed in a deep frown. "It's like you've become a different person. I don't think I can be friends with you right now."

I opened my mouth and shut it again. Linda was my last lifeline to the outside world. She was also someone who had clearly chosen to believe Rachel over me.

"I'm sorry," was all I said.

The end of that relationship took a toll on me. My best friend had simply dropped me, and I hadn't been able to stop it.

Weeks later, Trent saw me sitting on a bench near a building where we both had classes. I was sitting on my own, just staring into space. We'd been going to the same school for years, but I had shut him out of my life. I didn't want to have to explain what I was doing to anyone.

Trent sat down next to me, frowning. "Chikiya. Are you alright?"

I shrugged and looked down. In the dark place I was in, the last person I wanted to talk to was someone from my church. Someone who I felt might judge me.

He looked around, doubtless wondering why no one was sitting near me. He started to talk to me again, but I stood up.

"Trent—no. I don't want to talk right now, okay?" I knew that if I talked to him, all the grief would come rushing back. "I just—want to be alone."

Trent stood up and backed up from the bench very slowly. "I—okay. Okay, Chikiya."

Only when he turned and walked away did I sit back down.

By the end of my junior year of college, I'd hit rock bottom. I had no church, no friends, and no boyfriend. I was drinking and having sex to numb the pain, but neither of those things was really making me happy.

I was in a dark place.

I was on the road to disaster.

CHAPTER 12

I eventually left Bowie State altogether, transferring into all online classes. As my isolation grew deeper, I began to realize that I needed help.

This mode of grieving wasn't serving me. I'd shut myself from everyone and everything, but in reality, this only made me feel worse. The drinking and sex had only made me feel lonelier and driven me further away from the people I cared about.

I needed help.

I needed to get back to God.

I knew that studying the Bible needed to be part of my healing. It was the word of God, and God was the only person I felt I could trust right now. He was the most important person in my life, and He had given me the Bible to understand who he was, and also who I was in Him.

I began using the Internet to find Bible study aids and programs. I landed on a Bible study YouTube channel, whose owner posted weekly insight, exercises, and other tips for getting the most out of studying your Bible.

Inspired by her close relationship with God and her friendly attitude, I eventually began writing to the channel's owner.

I explained my situation to her: I'd spent years distancing myself from my Christian friends, and my old church no longer seemed to be the right place for me. Besides being the place where I'd met my abusive ex, its youth nights no longer seemed to hold anything new for me. I almost felt as though I had outgrown it.

It sounds like you could use some strong female fellowship, she told me. Don't worry. There are organizations that can help you.

She sent me a list of women's ministry groups around the country. These were groups run for women, by women, many of whom had experiences similar to mine.

They were concerned, not with meeting the world's standards, but with meeting God's. And that included loving one another, holding each other accountable, and refraining from judging each other.

Such a group sounded too good to be true. But we soon found a local chapter that met at a community center near me.

I knew as soon as I walked into the room that I was comfortable. More than a dozen young women around my age sat around a table. When I walked in, every single one of them looked up at me and smiled. One waved me over to join them, pulling an empty chair for me into their circle.

"Welcome," the girl to my left said. "What's your name?"

"Chikiya." I waved a little bit. I was self-conscious about everyone looking at me—but somehow, in a good way. It didn't feel like I would struggle to fit in here at all. It felt like I was important to them—but also like they would not judge me.

Looking around the circle, I could easily see myself in these other women. They were kind, well-meaning, friendly—but they were also college students and twenty-somethings, along with some older women. I realized they could just as easily have been through the same things I'd gone through.

Here I found many women who had walked the same path as me: women who had lost themselves trying to please men, or trying to keep them. Women who had not had the support and the courage to demand to be treated the way they deserved.

Women who had lost themselves in the world, and then found themselves in God.

They understood what sisterhood was. They understood that it was about acceptance *and* accountability. About giving people a safe place to land, *and* helping them stay on the right path.

I watched as other women in the group opened up about their journeys. Some wept as they spoke about their challenges with family, friends, and boyfriends. Some openly expressed their doubts and fears as they talked about their academics, career, and health challenges.

No thought seemed to be unsafe to express here—and the support included accountability. Your sisters in Christ wouldn't hesitate to tell you when you could be doing better for yourself.

In time, I began to open up to them. It felt so good to be understood. To feel accepted—not like you were in competition with anybody.

Having true sisters to walk with—sisters who shared a mutual friend in God—helped me to feel safe and open up as I had not in many years. Seeing that we had all gone through hard times and come out on the other side gave me confidence.

We all had the same goal in mind: to please God. Knowing this, I could rest easy in the knowledge that these women had my back.

The group's mission was to "honor God with our bodies, minds, and souls." From there, I made the decision to be abstinent again—just as I had been before losing my grandparents and Andy.

Now, I didn't need to worry about living by the world's standards to gain acceptance. I could be confident in my decision to live by God's.

Losing Linda was the first time that a friendship ending had hurt like a breakup. She had kept me company during the most difficult times, and in some ways, she was the last person I trusted not to judge me. With her gone, I was truly alone.

Alone with God.

The Bible teaches that you are never truly alone if you have a relationship with God. I'd believed that when I attended my old church. But somehow, I thought, as I slid into the ways of the world, that God wouldn't want me anymore. That even He would judge me for what I had done.

That was always the reason I closed myself off. I was afraid of being judged. By my family, by my friends, by my churchmates. Instead of baring my soul to them, I felt more comfortable shutting them out.

But now I was alone. I was desperate for company, and God was the one person who was supposed to always forgive.

God, why is this happening to me? I asked one night, sitting on the edge of my bed in the dark. *Why have my friends and boyfriends treated me like this? Why did I lose my grandparents, when I was just getting to know them?*

And I heard God say, *To learn lessons.*

What lessons, God? What good could possibly come out of all of this?

I began to question how I got here. Why was it that I, who only wanted friendship and affection, had ended up so very alone? Why had I so often felt unhappy even when I was in relationships?

I began to dissect my behavior. I had stayed with Jordan and Andy long after they began acting in ways that were uncomfortable to me. Why? Because I craved their love and approval. I was afraid of ending up alone if I didn't please them. And I felt that pleasing them was my job.

Pleasing them *was never your job, Chikiya,* I heard God say. *Your job was to please* me. *And you were never going to end up alone. I have always been with you.*

But I would also have been less anxious. I would have made wiser decisions if I had recognized that I wasn't alone—that the most important relationship of all was the Father who was always there with me.

Even when I was single, I wasn't alone. God was with me. And he was helping me learn who he had created me to be.

With Andy, maybe we just weren't the right match. Maybe *I* wasn't the right match for *him*. I had been so afraid of ending up alone that I didn't want him to talk to any other women. That had brought to light so many of my own insecurities. It had driven him away from me entirely, and I had ended up with what I most feared.

You didn't know your worth, God said. You worked so hard to prove yourself to them because you didn't know your worth.

You chased the approval of men—images of

Linda, Rachel, and Tisha flashed through my mind— *and friendships.*

I remembered how I had always felt *different.* How I'd felt that I stood apart because I didn't pursue men or dress provocatively. Because I didn't date often. How I'd felt pressured to change, to be more like the others. How I had clung to men who seemed to accept me as I was, even when it started to become clear that we weren't really that compatible.

You craved approval from the world, God said.

But you never needed their approval.

You always had mine.

The idea that *God himself* approved of me brought tears to my eyes. I'd learned in church about sin and forgiveness. I'd heard pastors say the *words* that "God's love is unconditional," but I now realized that I'd never really believed it. I had felt that avoiding sin meant I had to hide my sins from God. To not trust, or open up to the One who loved me most.

The relief I felt that night was immeasurable. But I still had a long way to go.

As I felt myself healing from my old fears and insecurities, I began to take my relationship with God much more seriously. I could feel His helpful presence now as never before. I became more active in my old church, and continued attending events with my women's ministry group.

One day in a discussion with a colleague from work, I found myself puzzled. The other person was saying something about the Bible that just didn't seem right to me, but I couldn't quite explain why.

I *did* know who knew the Bible better than almost anyone. I picked up the phone and dialed Tyrell's number.

"Chikiya?" He sounded a little bit unbelieving, and very happy to hear from me. Just like Trent, I'd lost touch with him during my last years at Bowie State. But I'd never deleted his number.

A big smile spread across my face. "Hi, Tyrell."

As we spoke on the phone that night, I felt like I saw him anew. We had known each other for years now, and they were years when we were growing fast.

Nothing could be the same now as it was in high school. I looked back on my own former relationships and felt just—puzzled. Why had I tolerated that behavior? Why had I acted that way myself? I remembered the fear of abandonment that had once roiled my stomach at the slightest sign of disapproval from a friend or family member.

Why had I felt that then?

Perhaps more to the point, why *didn't* I feel that now?

God was the ultimate reason, of course. The more I prayed and studied the Bible, the more I really did understand and perceive that He was always with me. I never walked alone.

My women's ministry sisters had been essential to the process, too. I now realized that had been one of my stumbling blocks growing up. There were ways I could not grow, a certainty I could not have, when I had never known real acceptance and love from the people around me.

Gaining acceptance and love was trickier than it seemed. I was beginning to understand this as I felt myself blossom under the sisterhood's support. My family loved me tremendously. But there was so much of myself I hadn't shown to them growing up. Those things I didn't show anybody—how could they ever be accepted, if nobody knew that they existed?

Nor could I just start showing my innermost fears and failings to just anyone. Being open with someone who would reject me might make the situation worse, as Jordan's betrayal made my fears worse in many ways.

I had needed the right people at the right time. God had led me to them, but their help was necessary for the process too.

I wondered if I sounded like I felt. Calmer, warmer, more loving because I was more secure. I wondered if I looked almost like a different person.

Tyrell had grown, too. He spoke like a professional now. His laughter no longer seemed boyish, but manly. In some ways, our changes were similar. Part of the manliness, I realized, was the steady calmness that came from no longer seeking approval. The confidence that came from knowing his abilities, his feelings, and his place in God's plan.

I wondered who had helped Tyrell grow, as the women's ministry had helped me. And so, I was thrilled when he invited me to his new church.

"It's really great, Chikiya," he told me. "The Spirit is very present. I've really been able to grow there. And Trent is a member, too."

Of course, I agreed to go with him.

Tyrell's new church was in Baltimore, Maryland. Tyrell and I had arrived early for the service, and the church was quiet. As soon as I walked in, I felt the Holy Spirit descend upon me.

I closed my eyes in the silence, dwelling in the peace and warmth. I could feel its strength filling me for the journey ahead.

And I heard God say: *This is your home now, Chikiya.*

I am still learning how God helps us grow through different situations. My stepmother's church, where I'd first met Trent and Tyrell, was a blessing and a necessary steppingstone. But now it was time for me to move on to a new place, with new lessons in store for me.

Trent greeted Tyrell and me with a big smile.

We were all growing together now, in a new place.

This story often felt rough while I lived it. I often asked God, "Why me?" when I was suffering from loneliness, insecurities, and feeling like my relationships just couldn't go right.

But now I know that everything that happened was part of my journey to get me to the place I am now. By going through these experiences, I've learned wisdom that I can share with others.

Is my life right now perfect? No. I still have my struggles. We will always have struggles, because that's the way we learn and grow. But through the trials of my teenage and college years, I grew in an important way: in my relationship with God.

Now I've learned to seek Him first above anyone or anything, in everything I do. I've learned that He is the one who loves us no matter what, and He is the one who knows what's best for our lives.

I want you to know that, regardless of where you come from, that doesn't have to be where you stay. You might be going through some very hard times right now, or you might have come from circumstances that seem hopeless.

They're not.

God will use any situation to His greater glory if you only work with him. He is there to teach you in every moment, and everything you learn from Him can make things better.

Even if you feel you have strayed too far from His flock, as I once did, He is out there looking for you. Jesus is the good shepherd who goes out to find the lost sheep, and He will always accept you back with open arms.

I've learned some very human lessons, as well as some divine ones, in my life. One of the most important is a lesson about friendship.

So often we feel like we have to please and try to fit in with anyone that we encounter in life. In reality, some people are better friends for us than others. We can do more of God's work, and have better lives for ourselves, if we choose our friends consciously.

Choose friends who treat you the way you *deserve* to be treated. If someone is mean to you, takes out their anger on you, or you notice that you always feel bad after spending time with them, you *don't* have to stick around.

Choose instead friends who uplift you and steer you toward Christ. I personally found my best friends in church: a place where most people agree that we should love one another, and hold each other accountable to good behavior.

Another important lesson I learned is both human and divine. I learned to forgive and pray for those who hurt me.

There were some people in this book who treated me pretty badly. They had unfair expectations of me, and acted in ways that were meant to be hurtful when I didn't meet them.

But in reality, they were struggling just like me. They probably felt insecure and unworthy, just like me. They were trying to fit in with the world, and they learned that that meant they "should" do certain things.

Jordan might have learned from the world that men are "supposed to" have a lot of sex, leading him to pressure and lie to me and other girls for sex in his effort to fit in with our culture's image of "the successful man."

My college friends may have learned what relationships are "supposed to be like" from media and movies, leading them to reject me when they felt that I wasn't meeting those expectations.

I got lucky. During the times when I felt so alone and rejected by other people, I was able to be alone with God. I was able to speak directly to our Creator in order to find myself and who I was.

What I learned was that we all struggle with the desire to fit in, and with expectations from our culture that are often toxic. I learned to understand the scripture that God gave me about forgiving and praying for those people who have caused me pain and heartache.

There is wisdom in the scripture that says, "Pray for your enemies." Your enemies aren't doing what they're doing because they're evil. They're doing it because they're scared, hurt, and don't understand.

Don't pray for their demise. Pray for their understanding. Pray that they might speak to God, like you have been able to, and that He will calm their hurt and pain. Pray that they will stop being afraid of not fitting in, and grow comfortable standing out.

I'm not nearly at the end of my journey. There are many more years of life ahead of me, which I know will be filled with more lessons. But the best any of us can do is to share what we've learned, in the hopes of helping someone else.

I continue to heal. I continue to work on myself. This is a constant process

It's a process that's constantly going on in your life, too.

I'll leave you with these questions to consider the next time you pray:

Where do you need healing?

What do you need to work on?

Who supports you when you're down?

Who *doesn't* treat you the way they should?

Remember that God will *always* treat you right, and that He is always there to talk when you need Him.

Be well. May we all walk the path together, holding each other's hands.

Made in the USA
Middletown, DE
03 March 2022

62010975R00102